It's fun to draw Ghosts and Ghouls

Mark Bergin

WINNIPEG
FEB 10 2015
PUBLIC LIBRARY

D1400960

Sky Pony Press
New York

Author:
Mark Bergin was born in Hastings, England. He has illustrated an award-winning series and written over twenty books. He has done many book designs, layouts, and storyboards in many styles including cartoon for numerous books, posters, and advertisments. He lives in Bexhill-on-sea with his wife and three children.

HOW TO USE THIS BOOK:
Start by following the numbered splats on the left-hand page. These steps will ask you to add some lines to your drawing. The new lines are always drawn in red so you can see how the drawing builds from step to step. Read the "You can do it!" splats to learn about drawing and shading techniques you can use.

Copyright © 2014 by Mark Bergin
First published in the UK by The Salariya Book Company ©
The Salariya Book Company Limited 2012.

All rights reserved. No part of this book may be reproduced in any manner without the express written consent of the publisher, except in the case of brief excerpts in critical reviews or articles. All inquiries should be addressed to Sky Pony Press, 307 West 36th Street, 11th Floor, New York, NY 10018.

Sky Pony Press books may be purchased in bulk at special discounts for sales promotion, corporate gifts, fund-raising, or educational purposes. Special editions can also be created to specifications. For details, contact the Special Sales Department, Sky Pony Press, 307 West 36th Street, 11th Floor, New York, NY 10018 or info@skyhorsepublishing.com.

Sky Pony® is a registered trademark of Skyhorse Publishing, Inc.®, a Delaware corporation.

Visit our website at www.skyponypress.com.

10 9 8 7 6 5 4 3 2 1

Manufactured in China, May 2014
This product conforms to CPSIA 2008

Library of Congress Cataloging-in-Publication Data is available on file.

Cover illustrations credit Mark Bergin

Print ISBN: 978-1-62914-611-9

PAPER FROM
SUSTAINABLE
FORESTS

Contents

4	Bat
6	Witch
8	Dragon
10	Monster
12	Ghost
14	Igor
16	Mummy
18	Scarecrow
20	Vampire
22	Werewolf
24	Witch on broomstick
26	Witch's cat
28	Wizard
30	Skeleton
32	Index

Bat

1 Start with the head shape.

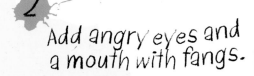

2 Add angry eyes and a mouth with fangs.

3 Draw in two pointed ears.

4 Add two wings.

splat-a-fact
Bats are the only mammals that can really fly.

you can do it!
Use a felt-tip marker for the lines and then add color with watercolor paints. Dab on more color with a sponge to add texture.

5 Draw in two legs and feet.

Witch

1 Start with this shape for the head and hat.

2 Draw in the peak of the witch's hat. Add the warty nose, mouth, teeth, and angry eyes.

Splat-a-fact
Witches make potions in their cauldrons and cast magic spells.

3 Add hair.

you can do it!
Use crayons to create swirly textures and paint over it with watercolor paint.

4 Draw in the body and the feet.

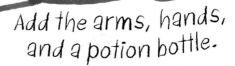

5 Add the arms, hands, and a potion bottle.

Dragon

1 Start with a
circle for the body.

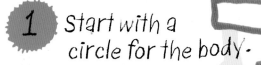

2 Draw in this head shape.

3 Add angry eyes, ears,
nostrils, and sharp teeth.

Splat-a-fact

Dragons scare off evil spirits.

4 Draw in two front legs.
and one back leg.

you can do it!

Use colored pencils. Put
textured surfaces under your
paper to create interesting
effects.

5 Add a wing and
a pointed tail.

8

9

Monster

Splat-a-fact

Frankenstein's monster has two bolts on his neck.

1 Start with a box-shaped head.

3 Add ears, hair, stitches, and bolts on the neck.

2 Draw in the eyes, nose, and mouth.

4 Add the body. Draw a curved line and button for his jacket.

5 Draw in the arms with a circle for each hand.

you can do it!

Use oil pastels, and smudge them with your finger. Use a felt-tip marker for the lines.

10

6 Add legs, feet, and ragged trousers.

Ghost

1 Cut out a wavy shape for the body. Glue down.

2 Draw in a mouth, and add two dots for the eyes.

you can do it!

Cut the shapes from colored paper and glue in place. Use a felt-tip marker for the lines.

splat-a-fact

Ghosts haunt old, spooky houses and come out at night.

MAKE SURE YOU GET AN ADULT TO HELP YOU WHEN USING SCISSORS!

3 Cut out two waving arms. Glue down.

Igor

2 Add two dots for the eyes. Draw in a bandage, a nose, ears, a mouth, and teeth.

splat-a-fact
Igor the monster is enormous!

1 Start with an oval shape for the head. Add tufts of hair.

3 Draw a circle for the body, and add a belt.

4 Add the arms with ragged sleeves.

you can do it!

Use a brown felt-tip marker for the lines and colored felt-tip markers to color in.

5 Draw in the legs and feet. Add trousers with ragged edges and a hole in them.

14

Mummy

1 Start with an oval for the head and dots for eyes.

2 Add bandages and a dot for the mouth.

3 Draw an oval for the body.

4 Add the arms.

5 Draw in two legs.

splat-a-fact

Mummies are wrapped in bandages and live in tombs.

6 Draw in the mummy's bandages.

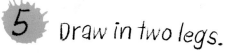

you can do it!

Use crayons to create textures and paint over it with watercolor paint. Use a felt-tip marker for the lines.

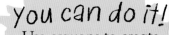

Scarecrow

you can do it!
Use a felt-tip marker for the lines and watercolor paints for color. Add ink to the paint while it is still wet for added interest.

1 Start with an oval for the head. Draw a line through the middle.

2 Add eyes, a nose, a jagged mouth, and a stalk.

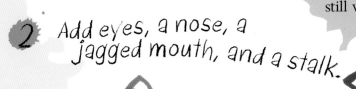

4 Draw in a jacket, belt, and frayed trousers. Add spiky straw feet.

3 Draw in curved lines.

splat-a-fact
Scary faces are carved into pumpkins on Halloween.

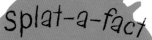

5 Add two arms and straw hands.

Vampire

Splat-a-fact

Vampires are afraid of sunlight and garlic.

1 Start with a circle for the head, and add two ears.

2 Draw in a nose, a mouth, fangs, and dots for the eyes. Add eyebrows and hair.

3 Draw in the body and arms. Add collar and necklace detail.

5 Add legs and feet.

4 Draw in the jacket, and add a cape.

you can do it!

Use a felt-tip marker for the lines and colored pencil to color in using scribbly marks.

20

Werewolf

you can do it!
Use colored pastel pencils and smudge the colors with your finger. Draw the lines with a felt-tip marker.

1 Start with this head shape.

2 Draw two angry eyes and nostrils. Add sharp teeth.

3 Add two front legs with furry paws.

4 Draw the back legs and bushy tail. Add a belt.

Splat-a-fact
Werewolves howl at the full moon.

22

23

Witch on broomstick

 1 Start with the witch's face. Draw a line for the hat.

 3 Draw in angry eyes, a mouth, and teeth. Add warts and hair.

2 Add the pointed hat.

splat-a-fact
Witches fly through the night on broomsticks.

4 Draw in the witch's tunic. Add arms and feet.

5 Add a broomstick.

you can do it!
Draw the outlines in a black felt-tip marker. Color in with colored pencils.

Witch's cat

you can do it!
Add color with
watercolor paint.

3 Add a pointy hat
and whiskers.

1 Start with an oval for
the head. Add the chin.

2 Draw in the eyes,
nose, and mouth.

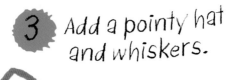

splat-a-fact
Witches have cats
to help them make
their potions.

4
Draw in two overlapping ovals
for the cat's body.

5 Add back and front legs
and a curved tail.

Wizard

MAKE SURE YOU GET AN ADULT TO HELP YOU WHEN USING SCISSORS!

1 Cut shapes for the head and hat. Glue down.

2 Cut a shape for the face, and glue down. Add eyes and a mouth with a felt-tip marker.

Splat-a-fact

Wizards can turn people into frogs with magic spells.

3 Cut out a tunic shape and triangles for feet. Glue down.

you can do it!

As you cut out the shapes, glue them down onto colored paper. Cut out simple shapes to make a bat and a frog.

4 Cut out the sleeves, hands, a wand, and a staff. Glue down.

28

Skeleton

1 Start with a skull shape.

2 Add eyes, a nose, and lines for the mouth.

3 Draw two ovals for the body. Add lines to one and two big dots to the other

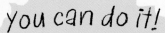

you can do it!
Color in with watercolor paint. Use a felt-tip marker for the lines.

4 Add bone shapes for the arms and hands.

Splat-a-fact
The smallest bone of the human body is found in the ear.

5 Draw in bone shapes for the legs.

Index

B
bat 4-5

C
crayon 6, 16

D
dragon 8-9

F
felt-tip marker 4, 10, 12, 14, 16, 20, 22, 24, 30

G
ghost 12-13

I
Igor 14-15
ink 18

M
monster 10-11
mummy 16-17

P
paint 4, 6, 16, 18, 26, 30

paper 10, 22
pastels 10, 22
pencils 8, 20, 22, 24

S
scarecrow 18-19
skeleton 30-31
smudging 10, 22
sponge 4

V
vampire 20-21

W
werewolf 22-23
witch 6-7
witch's cat 26-27
witch on broomstick 24-25
wizard 28-29